For Saskia
M.W.

ISBN 0-439-13315-7

Text copyright © 1999 by Martin Waddell.
Illustrations copyright © 1999 by Barbara Firth.
All rights reserved.
Published by Scholastic Inc., 555 Broadway, New York, NY 10012,
by arrangement with Candlewick Press.
SCHOLASTIC and associated logos are trademarks
and/or registered trademarks of Scholastic Inc.

12 11 10 9 8 7 6 5 4 3 2 1   9/9 0 1 2 3 4/0

Printed in the U.S.A.   14

First Scholastic printing, October 1999

This book was typeset in Monotype Columbus.
The pictures were done in pencil and watercolor.

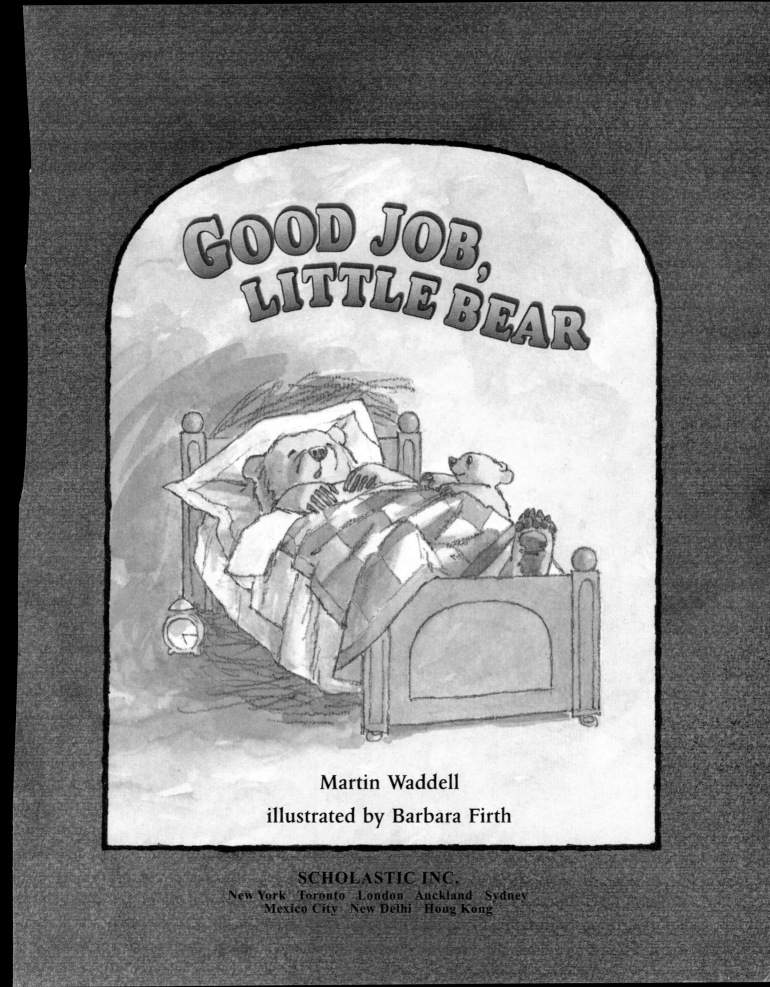

GOOD JOB, LITTLE BEAR

Martin Waddell

illustrated by Barbara Firth

SCHOLASTIC INC.
New York Toronto London Auckland Sydney
Mexico City New Delhi Hong Kong

. . . always."

Big Bear and Little Bear settled down,

cozy and warm in the Bear Chair.

"Were you scared, Little Bear?" asked Big Bear.

"Were you scared when you fell in the water?"

"I knew you'd be there," Little Bear said.

"That's right, Little Bear," said Big Bear.

"I'll be there when

you need me . . .

Big Bear and Little Bear explored

their way home through the woods,

all the way back to the Bear Cave.

"Let's go exploring some more,

   Little Bear," said Big Bear.

"Exploring where?" Little Bear asked.

"On the far side of the stream," said Big Bear.

"Take care, Big Bear, you might fall

   in like me," Little Bear said.

"Not if you show me the stone

   where you slipped," said Big Bear.

      "It was this stone," Little Bear said.

         "Good job, Little Bear!"

            said Big Bear.

Big Bear waded in, and he pulled

Little Bear out of the water.

"Don't cry, Little Bear," Big Bear said.

"We'll soon have you dry."

He hugged Little Bear.

"Help me, Big Bear,"

Little Bear cried.

"Take care, Little Bear," said Big Bear.

"I am taking care," Little Bear said.

"Little Bear . . . !"

called Big Bear . . .

Little Bear hopped from one stone to another.

"I'm the best hopper there is!" Little Bear said.

Little Bear hopped again,

and again.

Little Bear found the stream near the shady place.

"I'm going over the stream," Little Bear said.

"Look at me, Big Bear. Look at me crossing

the stream by myself."

"Good job, Little Bear,"

said Big Bear.

right into the arms of Big Bear.

"You caught me again!" Little Bear said.

"Good job, Little Bear," said Big Bear.

"I'm going exploring some more!"

Little Bear said.

"Are you ready, Big Bear?"
Little Bear called to Big Bear.

Little Bear bounced

higher and higher,

and he bounced

off the branch . . .

Little Bear bounced on the branch.

"Watch me bounce higher,

Big Bear!" Little Bear said.

"Well done, Little Bear," said Big Bear.

Little Bear found

the old bendy tree.

"Look at me!" Little Bear said.

"I'm bouncing about

on the old bendy tree!"

"I need you now, Big Bear,"

Little Bear shouted. "I'm jumping."

"I'm here, Little Bear," said Big Bear.

Little Bear jumped off Bear Rock

into the arms of Big Bear.

"I'm off exploring again!"

Little Bear said, and he ran

on in front of Big Bear.

Little Bear found Bear Rock.

"Look at me!" Little Bear said.

"Where are you, Little Bear?" asked Big Bear.

"I'm exploring Bear Rock,"

Little Bear said. "Watch me climb."

"Good job, Little Bear,"

said Big Bear.

Once there were two bears,

Big Bear and Little Bear.

Big Bear is the big bear

and Little Bear is the little bear.

One day, Little Bear wanted

to go exploring.

Little Bear led the way.